Solo

Paul Geraghty

Crown Publishers, Inc. *New York*

To the high-flying businessman
and her cat

Published in the United States of America by Crown Publishers, Inc.,
a Random House company, 201 East 50th Street, New York, NY 10022.
Originally published in Great Britain in 1995 by Hutchinson Children's Books.

CROWN is a trademark of Crown Publishers, Inc.

Manufactured in Hong Kong

Library of Congress Cataloging-in-Publication Data
Geraghty, Paul.
Solo / written and illustrated by Paul Geraghty.
p.   cm.
Summary: When her parents Floe and Fin leave her to search for food,
Solo the baby penguin tries to follow and loses her way.
1. Penguins—Juvenile fiction. [1. Penguins—Fiction.] I. Title
PZ10.3.G3355So   1996
[E]—dc20   95-13821

ISBN 0-517-70908-2 (trade)
0-517-70909-0 (lib. bdg.)

10 9 8 7 6 5 4 3 2 1

First Edition

In the dark of winter,
Floe leapt out of the sea.

For days she hiked across the ice. It blew and
it snowed. She slid and she stumbled, but she
never once stopped to rest.

Sometimes she tobogganed; often she
had to climb.

She was on her way to meet her mate, Fin.

Just as the struggle began to seem endless,
Floe's heart quickened. She could hear a
great noise in the distance.

Up ahead, the horizon was dark with
penguins gathering in the thousands. The
colony grew and grew, with more arriving
each minute. She was nearly home.

Floe bustled through the rookery, calling for Fin. If he'd survived the months at sea, he would be here somewhere, looking for her too.

For hours she called. Then, far away in the forest of noise, she thought she heard him. She called, then listened. Faintly, his voice echoed back. It was Fin!

Floe called again. Fin replied. She followed
the sound she knew so well.

    And there he was at last. They bowed
and stretched with delight. They touched
chests. Fin led Floe on a celebration walk.
They were together again.

A few weeks later, their voices sang out
with pride. Floe had laid her egg.
She passed it to Fin. He took it
onto his feet, gently covered
it against the cold, and
prepared for the
long, hungry
wait.

Again they sang, and then Floe was gone—on the
long journey back to the sea to collect food for
the baby.

At the water's edge she hesitated. She was
desperate to swim, but something made her stop.

Then she saw it...

… a leopard seal! Just beneath the ice, ready to snatch her as she dived in. Floe stood still and waited.

Eventually, the seal flicked the surface and set off, looking for less careful penguins to hunt.

Floe splashed into the clear water and twisted down into the deep.

Back in the rookery, Fin
huddled with the
other penguins to
keep warm.
For three bitter
months, he had
been without
food, and
still he
protected
the egg.

Then, one
morning, he
heard a tapping
sound. Slowly, the
egg began to crack.
Fin watched in wonder
as the shell broke open
and the baby was born.
The first thing baby Solo
saw was a winter storm.

Floe wasn't back from the sea, so Fin fed her what little oil he had.

Excitement grew as the first fat females returned. All around them, other chicks were starting to hatch.

At last Floe arrived. The sight of Fin with baby Solo filled her with joy. She bowed and bumped against Fin. He passed her the baby. They showed cheeks and sang, and Solo got her first good meal of squid.

Then, desperate with hunger,
Fin set straight off for the sea.
It was his turn to collect
the food.
    He splashed with delight.
He tumbled and swam. For weeks
he dived and fished.

At the rookery, Solo was growing well. Floe had run out of food, but Fin was a good diver. He'd soon be back with plenty of squid. Then she could go fishing again.

One morning, Floe and Solo saw dark shapes approaching in the distance—fat, waddling penguins! They could hardly wait.

But Fin wasn't among the first ones back. They could only watch as all around them chicks were fed and hungry mothers were finally free to go to sea.

Each time more penguins arrived, their spirits rose. But still Fin didn't come.

Days passed. Anxiously, they watched as the last few stragglers came home. Perhaps Fin had gotten lost? Or had he gone farther than the others to find good food?

Solo cried with hunger, but Floe had nothing left to feed her. She was hungry too. And now there were no more shapes in the distance to give them hope.

Floe waited one more day. When Fin didn't come, she knew she would have to leave her chick, or they would both starve. She put Solo on the snow, looked back once, then hurried off toward the sea. It was a faint hope, but perhaps she could make the trip in time to save her chick.

Solo tried to follow, but she couldn't keep up. She waited quietly for a while, but then she cried from the cold.

A few heads turned. Some of the penguins noticed that Solo was on her own.

One penguin tried to drag her onto his feet, but another pulled her from behind. A third tugged at her flipper. Suddenly, five large penguins were fighting over Solo. They all wanted to care for her, but they tugged and nipped so hard that she cried out with fright.

Scurrying away, Solo slid
down a crevice. At the
bottom she lay awhile,
panting with shock. Curious
faces peered down at her.
At least she was safe
from their jabbing beaks.

Slowly she recovered, and soon had the strength
to struggle along the bottom. At one end, the space
opened up, and Solo found herself at the edge of the
rookery. From there, she set off to find her mother.

She hadn't gone far when a great bird, a skua, swooped
down, knocking her to the ground. She cried, trying to
get up; then a gust of wind blew her down again, bowling
her over and over. The wind blew harder. She rolled and
slid along the ice.

The skua fought the wind, waiting to dive again.

Solo called for her mother, but Floe was far away,
still hurrying to the sea. She struggled to her feet
and looked back. The rookery was out of sight.

A bitter wind bowled her over again. And this time she
didn't get up. She lay on the ice, weak and shivering.
    The skua landed and settled its wings, ready
for an easy meal. It reached forward, nipped at
Solo's belly, and began to tug.
    Solo cried out...

...and a passing shape stopped. It hobbled over and lunged at the skua.

Fin was back!

He had finally completed his journey, dragging a fisherman's net the whole way with him.

Weeks later, to Fin and Solo's delight, they
heard a familiar sound across the icy wastes–
a halfhearted call from Floe.

   At once they both replied. And for a wonderful
moment they listened to Floe getting closer, calling
with joy and disbelief.